Hope

Carole J Lisson

WestBow Press books may be ordered through booksellers or by contacting:

WestBow Press
A Division of Thomas Nelson & Zondervan
1663 Liberty Drive
Bloomington, IN 47403
www.westbowpress.com
1 (866) 928-1240

ISBN: 978-1-9736-3810-0 (sc)
ISBN: 978-1-9736-3811-7 (e)

Library of Congress Control Number: 2018909334

Print information available on the last page.

WestBow Press rev. date: 09/13/2018

WESTBOW
PRESS®
A DIVISION OF THOMAS NELSON
& ZONDERVAN

The story of "Hope" is just that. Carole Lisson has weaved a wonderful tale of a dog named Hope, who serves as a wonderful introductory allegory for children (and their parents!) of the hope the Savior of the world brings to all who will receive His hard-won gift of salvation. My daughter and I both enjoyed reading about this hope for which we all long.

—*Kevin Conway (PhD Cambridge) - Theological Trainer in Eastern Europe & Russia for Campus Crusade for Christ*

As a parent, grandparent, and Sunday school teacher I sometimes found it a challenge to explain to children, in an understandable manner, the complex concept of the Greatest Story ever told. In this book, Carole Lisson tells the delightful, heartwarming story of Charity and her dog, Hope. After reading this allegory to children, it will be an easy transition to turn the discussion to the sacrifice of Jesus Christ. Thanks Carole!

—*Mark Motluck. Professor Emeritus, Anderson University, B.B.A., M.B.A.. J.D.*

I sat down to read Carole Lisson's book, <u>Hope,</u> this evening not knowing what to expect. I knew it was a children's book so I thought it might be a simple Gospel story geared towards young minds. Instead I was surprised how quickly it captivated my middle-aged mind and heart. Many of us are dog-lovers and you will immediately identify with the main character's desire to own her own dog. As you follow the story you are drawn into the growing friendship between a young girl and her dog. They go through everyday situations together; school, bullies, playing the park, and even a frightening visit to the Vet. As the story unfolds adults will begin to see the deeper meaning. They will find that this allegorical story is an excellent way to bring up many Gospel truths with children. The necessity and sufficiency of Christ's atoning sacrifice on the cross is one of those truths that can be discussed after reading this story. There is also an easy link that can be made from the story to the need for repentance and faith in Jesus Christ. So thank you Carole for making this teaching tool available to both parents and those ministering to young hearts!

—Rev. Michael J. Walsh, B.A. Moody Bible Institute, M.A.
Columbia Biblical Seminary. Michael has been serving
as a missionary in Ireland for the last 28 years.

I absolutely loved this book! It brought tears to my eyes as I read the story of Hope's love and sacrifice! This book is an amazing way to share Jesus with children!

—Lois Linnane
Coordinator of Evangelism & Outreach Influence Leader,
Wheaton Bible Church & Tri-Village Church

Foreword:

Confession: I often skip forwards because I'm eager to get to the story. But I am asking you, dear reader, to skip all the way to the back of this book to read the last paragraphs in the Acknowledgements. It includes my thank you to Jesus, the reason for this allegory. Then I might ask that you "cheat" and read the teacher/parent notes pointing out some similarities and dissimilarities the story contains. That way, as you read this to young ones you can assist them in their understanding. God bless you!

Charity's Desire

Charity was a young girl who wanted a dog so badly her heart ached. This longing hurt because she knew it could never happen since she had severe dog allergies. She itched, sneezed and got a scratchy throat when a dog even came near her, so owning one was out of the question. Even so, Charity secretly prayed for a miracle every Christmas that she would somehow have her very own dog one day.

Desire Becomes Hope

Just a week before Christmas, out of the blue, a dog showed up at Charity's front door. Charity looked out through the glass into his beautiful face that seemed to say, "Hi, I'm your new best friend." Charity's heart skipped a beat.

In her excitement, she forgot about her allergies and hurried out to hug him. He nuzzled her affectionately right back. Charity thought she would burst with joy. She wasn't sneezing, itching or getting stuffed up! Charity wasn't the least bit allergic to him. *Oh goodness, she thought, I wonder if my mom and dad will allow me to keep him?* She called her mom and dad to come and see who had arrived. Charity was certain he was there to be adopted and that God had heard her prayers.

Her parents were less optimistic. They knew Charity wanted to keep him but explained even though she didn't seem allergic to him, he might just be lost and his owners would be looking for him. But they agreed that, if after alerting the shelters, he wasn't claimed in two weeks, she could keep him. Charity whispered to her new best friend, "I'll call you Hope, as in, ***I hope*** I can keep you!"

Joy and Patience

Over the next two weeks the two were inseparable. It was as though Hope could read Charity's mind. When she felt like playing, he'd run get a baseball. When she needed to read, he'd lay at her feet quietly.

Other times, after a long day, Charity enjoyed resting on Hope's chest as she listened to his heartbeat. He was the best thing that ever happened to her.

Hope = Love

After fourteen days, Charity ran home from school as fast as she possibly could. "Well? Has anyone claimed him?" she blurted. Her mom and dad smiled. "Charity, Hope is all yours! Looks like it was meant to be!"

Charity jumped for joy. After she thanked God for the best parents ever, she thanked Him for the best gift she could imagine. Hope jumped on Charity, making her laugh. The whole family was pretty much over the moon with joy.

Best Buds

It was soon very clear that this rather common looking dog was no ordinary canine. He was super-duper, crazy smart. No one had ever seen such a well behaved, obedient dog. He protected Charity from dangers she didn't even know were there. He appeared to have super powers that completely set him apart from other dogs.

Hope and Charity enjoyed each season together. He pulled her on a sled in the winter and pulled her on her skateboard in the spring. On hot summer days, they swam together at a nearby pond. When Charity got tired she could just hang on Hope's neck. He was so strong he could hold her up and swim at the same time.

People would go to their windows whenever Charity and Hope were going by their houses because they were such a fun sight to see.

Secret Language

Hope and Charity had a secret language. When Hope wanted to say "Yes," he would put his right paw on her knee. And when Hope needed to say "I'll be right back," he would put his left paw on her knee. Charity could ask "Hey Hope, do you want to play frisbee?" and he would put his right paw on her knee and off they'd go. But often Hope had missions he'd need to dash off to and that's when he'd use his left paw saying *gotta run but I'll be right back.* Through his doggy door he'd run to help someone in need.

Hope Saves the School

On one of his rescue missions, Hope saved the school from a fire. He would go with Charity to school and since dogs weren't allowed inside he'd wait by the flag pole for her. But one day in the middle of class Charity heard Hope barking loud and shrill. She knew this was his danger bark. Charity yelled, "We have to get out of the school immediately!" The teacher believed her and pulled the fire alarm and the whole school got out in time.

Once all were safe a Firefighter placed a hat on Hope's head and they all had a much needed laugh. From that point on Hope the hero was asked to sit next to Charity in class.

Jealous Bullies

All the attention after the fire rescue was the last straw for some bullies who were already jealous of Charity and Hope. They were furious that Hope was allowed to sit next to Charity in school even though it was for their protection too. Though many in town loved Hope and Charity, this group of meanies were just seething with envy at their increased popularity.

The bullies had expensive, fancy dogs who were also jealous. Envious of Hope's uncanny rescue powers, they made fun of how common he looked. The owners and their pedigreed dogs hated Charity and Hope. Tears ran down Charity's cheeks as she wrote her feelings in her journal one evening. She also noted how their comments didn't faze Hope. He loved everyone, even those who were mean to them. Charity wanted to be more like Hope but it wasn't easy.

Hope Rescues Bully

One evening, Hope was lying under the table while Charity was doing her homework. Suddenly Hope's ears perked up. He put his left paw on Hope's knee (saying he'd be right back) and took off through his doggy door. He returned about a half hour later and went back to lying quietly under the table.

The next day Charity found out Hope had run several miles to the home of one of the bullies to rescue her from choking. He pounced on her back to dislodge a piece of candy. The bully's fancy dog stood by helpless having no idea what to do. That was all it took to change this bully's mind about Hope and Charity. She and her dog became instant friends with them both. She even apologized for being so mean. Charity and Hope forgave them eagerly and they were all great pals from that day forward.

Mad-dog Strikes

Then something bizarre started to happen. Many dogs began getting a disease they named "Mad-dog." Their fur fell out and they became aggressive, unpredictable and started to bite. Others just lay around lethargic and "sick as dogs"! There were news reports that Mad-dog was spreading very quickly and dogs were dying.

It spread throughout the county, then the state, then the whole country! Soon it had spread throughout the entire world! All the dogs were dying. If something wasn't done quickly there would be *no more dogs on planet earth!*

But Charity saw that Hope didn't have any symptoms. Hope wasn't losing his fur and was as obedient and attentive as ever. What was going on? Somehow word got out that Hope didn't have Mad-dog. He was the only healthy dog on earth.

Hope Is The Only Hope

Some men from the local clinic knocked on Charity's door. They wanted to examine Hope since he had no signs of Mad-dog. They said they would test his blood in order to make a serum that would possibly save other dogs' lives. Charity hesitated. She didn't know if she trusted these men. Hope looked at her and put his right paw on her knee and then his left. He was saying "yes" to their request, and adding "I'll be right back." She completely trusted Hope's instincts so she said okay.

The men took Hope away. Charity waited for hours for them to return, and when they didn't, she became worried. She finally asked her parents to take her to the clinic where the men had taken Hope. The attendants at the door wouldn't let her in so she peeked into a basement window. There she saw Hope lying on a cold, stainless steel table just as he was about to be shaved.

She screamed and ran to her parents.

When they got back to the window they saw that poor Hope had been shaved. As they looked more closely they saw he was covered with needle marks. Then Charity realized with horror his chest wasn't going up and down. "HE'S NOT BREATHING!" she screamed. "They killed him! They murdered him! **He's dead!"**

"THEY KILLED MY HOPE!"

Death, Unbearable Grief

Charity buried herself in her parents' arms. She was confused and shouted angrily to her parents. "Did they infect him with the Mad-dog disease and it killed him? What did they do to him? They said they needed his blood but they didn't tell me he would have to die. All he ever did was help people. They killed him to save these spoiled rotten, disobedient dogs! They tricked me! Those foolish bullies ought to be happy now. There will be no one to rescue them or anyone else in this stupid town when trouble comes!" she sobbed.

When Hope Becomes Reality

Charity questioned God. Why would He answer her prayers for a dog only to have Hope then killed? As she lay on her bed she replayed the last thing Hope did. He put **both** paws on her knee. The right paw to say yes he'd go with those bad men and the left to say he'd be back. Hope had never misled her before. She could always trust him. *Could Hope save everyone but himself with his super powers?* Charity wondered.

Her heart was shattered and she was certain it would never be whole again.

Charity sobbed herself into a sound sleep. She was dreaming that Hope was alive and they were playing again. She dreamed he was licking her face. Gradually, as she awoke, she realized her face was wet because it **was actually Hope licking her face for real! He was alive!**

What in the world? Hope was staring at her and she knew she wasn't dreaming when he barked his happy bark. **He DID come back just as he said!** He was as alive as ever! *He really does have super powers,* Charity realized. He's no ordinary dog!

How in the world did this happen? How did he even get in her room when her door was shut? Charity jumped out of bed and went absolutely crazy with joy! Hope jumped up and they danced together. His fur was all grown back and he looked beautiful. Charity didn't know this much joy was possible.

The End

Or...is...it?

Now that Charity had stopped mourning and was finally able to go outside again, she thought she'd see everyone rushing to get the serum that would save their dogs' lives. But to her shock, not that many were going. "What!?" she asked. "Hope sacrificed himself to make this serum and yet some of you aren't going to get it? *Why?*" She begged people, even the bullies, to go to the clinic because they were giving out free inoculations. "They will even come to your house if your dog is too sick to get there," she explained to them. "All you have to do is ask."

Thankfully, some owners did hurry to get it, but most just thought it was silly and that it wouldn't work. So they risked their dogs' lives out of their stubbornness? *That made no sense!*

Charity, now joined by her parents and several others who had gotten the serum for their dogs, pleaded with people to get it. But the doubters alleged, "Well look at your dogs who got the serum. They don't look all that different than ours, so it must not work!" Charity said, "That's because it takes time! The serum doesn't work overnight. But as soon as they're injected you can be sure they won't die of Mad-dog."

Look at Hope. He was dead and now he's alive! They exposed him to Mad-dog and he conquered it and even came back to life! Can't you just trust me and get the injection? It's free! Please?"

Some did and some didn't. Why do you think that is?

What do you think you would do?

Important teacher/parent suggestion: If this story is too long to read in a classroom setting or Bible club I _would highly recommend learning the story_ in advance and only glancing at the subtitles or photos so you can tell it in your own words. Practice your paraphrasing several times before you present it. This will help you maintain eye contact with the kids and use appropriate expressions as you go.

Notes:

*Discuss how Hope represents Jesus. See similarities and dissimilarities below.

*This is called an **allegory** because it's a story with a deeper or hidden meaning.

*If your listeners are very young simply explain the meaning.

Did you find at least 9?

1. **Jesus** appeared on the scene 2000 years ago. He was **hoped for** but still **unexpected.** He was the fulfillment of Scripture, but especially for those who were waiting for the Messiah, the Promised One (Simeon and Anna for example in Luke 2:25-38). Hope also appeared on the scene suddenly, hoped for but still unexpected.

2. **Jesus' mission was to save and serve.** During His three years of public ministry He healed, taught and served people. The last verse in the book of John (written by Jesus' best friend) said that if everything Jesus did were written down the whole world couldn't contain the books that would be written. In a similar way, Hope's main purpose was to save dogs from death caused by Mad-dog, but until that time came he was always helping, rescuing and serving.

3. **Our sin infected all of mankind from the moment it entered the world** through Adam and Eve, our first representatives (Romans 3:23). We didn't "catch it" like the dogs in the story caught Mad-dog, we were born with it. We inherit a sin nature at birth that makes us spiritually dead (Romans 6:23). As Hope sacrificed himself to make the serum, Jesus sacrificed Himself on the cross to pay for our sin (2 Cor. 5:21). There was enough serum to save all the dogs but not all of them received the free gift. Jesus' blood is sufficient to cover the sins of all Mankind (Hebrews 10:10), yet not everyone accepts the free gift that He offers (Romans 6:26;

Ephesians 2 :8,9; Matthew 7:13). Of course, Jesus' death was far more horrible and painful than Hope's. Excruciating means "from the cross." The scourging, whipping, mocking, nails and torturous crucifixion were agony beyond what we can imagine. But being separated from His Father for the first time in all of eternity was the worst pain of all. That is the only time Jesus cried out in pain, "Father, why have You forsaken me?" (Matthew 27:46). The Father had to turn away from His only Son as He bore our sin because Holiness cannot be intimate with sin. As Jesus bore all the past, present and future sin of all mankind, His Father had to withdraw from Him and Jesus was alone. That caused Jesus to cry out in agony. He'd never been without His Father until that moment. Jesus alone paid the penalty for our sin debt and He paid it in full (John 19:30). All that's left for us to do is to believe and receive. Believe that Jesus really is God and paid the penalty for yours and my sin and receive His free gift of living with Him forever and ever so we never really die from our sin (Mad-dog) as we deserve. The dogs in the story did nothing to earn the serum. Hope alone willingly made the sacrifice and made it possible for them to live. All the owners and their dogs needed to do was believe enough to receive it (Ephesians 2:8,9).

4. **Only Jesus** was **qualified to be** the **Father's acceptable sacrifice** for us because His sinlessness meant His blood was Holy. Only Hope was qualified to make the serum because he had pure, uninfected (by Mad-dog) blood (1 Peter 1:19).

   *Have you ever wondered how the **disciples** might have **felt** when Jesus, their "Hope," was crucified? Anger? Confusion? Fear? Grief? Horror? After Hope's death Charity displayed a **range of** those **emotions** at losing her Hope.

5. **Jesus died and was buried** in a rich man's grave as prophesied. But **then! He rose from the dead** to prove He really did conquer sin and death. He was seen by over 500 people to prove He was telling the truth all along (1 Cor. 15:1-11) that He is God just as He claimed to be and did exactly what He said He would do (John 2:19-22). Hope too came back to life, conquering Mad-dog and even appearing in Charity's room without coming through the door. Did you know Jesus did that too? After He rose from the dead, He suddenly appeared midst his fearful disciples who were huddled in a door-locked room (John 20:19).

6. The reason fewer were going to get the serum than would be expected represents the wide and narrow path. Those who got the serum were like those who trust in Jesus for their salvation and therefore **enter through the narrow gate, for the gate is broad that leads to destruction** and there are many who enter through it (Matt. 7:13). Most people will not receive the free gift of salvation just as most did not get the serum.

7. **When we are saved the sanctification process begins.** God will complete this process instantly when we die. His word states that He Himself will complete the work He began in us (Phil. 1:6). The key is that while we're still on earth we're in process. We don't instantly reflect Christ-like character the moment we're saved. That takes time and because of that, the unbelieving world can often be confused by us. We believers still sin and aren't instantly healed of our sin nature when we become followers of Jesus. Something similar happened in the story. Many used the excuse not to get the serum because the dogs who received it weren't that different. Charity tried to explain it takes time. We try to explain that to non-believers too. Please don't judge Jesus (Hope) by His followers (the dogs who received the serum). We are under construction until God completes His work in us. The dogs who were healed in the story will eventually die. We, however, who are saved, will not. Yes, our bodies will die but our souls will live forever. For believers, the moment we die we will be in the presence of Jesus. When Jesus returns we will all get new bodies (2 Corinthians 5:1-10). These bodies will actually resemble the ones we have now in the sense we will recognize each other. However, our new bodies will be incorruptible. That means they will never get sick, never age, never get cancer, never need glasses, never have diseases and so on. They will be perfect and will last forever and ever.

8. **Jesus was not handsome**. The prophet Isaiah tells us, **"There was nothing about His physical appearance that would attract people to Him,** yet people were drawn to Him because of His character." (Isaiah 53:2). Jesus' holy character was both a compelling draw to people and a source of holy fear. The different responses to Hope in the story are reminders of **our** different **responses to Jesus**. Some of us look on with wonder like those looking out their windows while others are intimidated and therefore critical. The owners and their "pedigreed fancy dogs" represent this group who were like the Pharisees who looked good on the outside but inside were hard-hearted. The Pharisees were jealous of Jesus and how the people followed Him and believed in Him which diminished their authority and favor with the people. The bullies and their fancy dogs were jealous too. Hope was not a "fancy" dog in appearance but his character, his devotion, love, loyalty, intelligence and obedience made him the most attractive dog ever.

9. **Charity represents** those of **us** who walk imperfectly but dependently through this life with Jesus. Her relationship with Hope is how Jesus wants us to be with Him. He longs to be our best friend. He is loving and devoted not only to us but to all who come to Him for forgiveness (Romans 10:13; Matt. 11:28; 1 John 1:9).

(There are more. I hope you find them.)

Acknowledgements:

Thank you to Betty Schuck for staging the photos and skillfully transforming them into "paintings." You made this story come alive. Also, thank you for spending *many hours* painstakingly editing and patiently teaching me Google docs operations in the process.

Thank you to the Wheaton Bible Awana girls and Neighborhood Bible Club kids whose precious faces I can still see while I told, or should I say attempted to tell this story. Every time I got to the part about Hope putting his right paw on Charity's knee I broke down. The reality of Jesus saying He'd go to the cross was too real and I'd lose it. Some of the kids just stared sympathetically and others cried with me. But they all waited patiently until I composed myself and finished with the good news. Each time some would ask for a copy of this story but one only existed in my head. Finally, their sweet requests motivated me to get in it writing.

Thank you to Rachael Farrell, for her great patience in modeling as Charity for the illustrations.

Thank you to Deb, Rebecca and Sarah Jean Farrell for their advanced read and input.

Thank you to Carol and Bill Blackburn for their read through and giving wise and encouraging feedback.

Thank you to Tiffany Richardson for your careful editing and punctuation corrections. Thank you for your valuable suggestions on content clarification. Thank you to Cora whose questions helped me "hear" this with the astute ears of an eight-year-old.

Thank you to Greg Lisson for training his dog Sam to be the "model" as Hope and contributing photos all the way from Wesleyan in Atlanta, GA.

Thank you to Sam whose beauty should have disqualified him for the part but his obedience, willingness and availability made him first choice.

Thank you to Sarah Lisson-Gemmel, Dave Lisson and Kathy Burke for the valuable suggestions.

And finally, thank You Jesus for making the good news a reality.

Bushels of gratitude to Bev Ruby for her eagle-eyed editing and unwavering support!

Could there be a more understated word for this news? It's so much more than **good.** Let me be blunt. I come from a family of exaggerators. I've worked on accurate reporting and eliminating hyperbole from my speech. So it's a great relief to relax knowing I simply cannot overstate the glorious goodness of this news. It's magnificent, mind-blowing, jaw-dropping, astonishing and breathtakingly amazing news! Through You, Jesus, we have a way to get to heaven. You, the God-man, set aside Your glory and privilege to come to this cesspool of sin, earth. You lived a sinless life and then willingly went to the cross to die a horrific death to pay for my sin; for all of our sin. You did that because You love us. Then You were put in a grave and rose from the dead to prove You really were Who You said You were. You told us if we believed in You, we could be with You in paradise forever. Lord Jesus, I believe in You with all my heart. And I can't wait to meet You in Person. I hope everyone reading this will put their faith in You this very moment so I get to meet them in heaven one day too.

If, like the thief at the cross (who received Jesus in the 11th hour), it's the last thing we ever do it will surely be the wisest thing we ever did.

CPSIA information can be obtained
at www.ICGtesting.com
Printed in the USA
LVHW052350060919
630250LV00005B/44/P

9 781973 638100